Naptime

Featuring Jim Henson's Sesame Street Muppets

By Anna Ross • Illustrated by Norman Gorbaty

Random House / Children's Television Workshop

Library of Congress Cataloging-in-Publication Data:
Ross, Anna. Naptime : featuring Jim Henson's Sesame Street Muppets / by Anna Ross ; illustrated by Norman Gorbaty. p. cm.–(A Sesame Street toddler book) SUMMARY: Little Big Bird would rather play with his friends than take a nap. ISBN: 0-394-85828-X [1. Naps (Sleep)–Fiction. 2. Sleep–Fiction. 3. Puppets–Fiction] I. Gorbaty, Norman, ill. II. Title. III. Series. PZ7.R71962Nap 1990 [E]–dc20 89-34545

Manufactured In Italy 4 5 6 7 0 9 0

Naptime, Little Big Bird.

"No nap. I want to climb with Grover."

But Little Grover is going to take his nap now...

Naptime, Little Big Bird.
"No nap. I want to finger-paint
with Bert."

But Little Bert has washed his hands
and is going to take his nap now…

Naptime, Little Big Bird.
"No nap. I'm looking for Ernie.
We're playing hide-and-seek. Oh, Ernie,
where are you?"

Little Ernie is under his covers, taking his nap. Doesn't that sound cozy?

Naptime, Little Big Bird.
"No nap. I want a cookie."

You and Little Cookie Monster may have cookies when you wake up from your naps.

Naptime, Little Big Bird.
"No nap. I'm going to
show this book to Betty Lou."
Little Betty Lou is going
beddy-bye, Little Big Bird.
And now it's time for you to
do the same.

"But I can't take a nap. I might miss something wonderful and exciting."

You won't miss anything exciting, Little Big Bird. Everybody else is taking a nap, too.

Little Grover is taking a nap…

and Little Bert is taking a nap...

and Little Ernie is taking a nap...

and Little Cookie Monster is taking
a nap...

and Little Betty Lou is taking a nap
too. What about you?

Aren't you a little sleepy? After all, you've been very busy. You've been climbing and painting and playing hide-and-seek and reading and...

Have a nice nap, Little Big Bird.